Stories of Sages and Sibyls

Stories

of

Sages

and

Sibyls

George Bothamley

Matador
9 Priory Business Park,
Wistow Road, Kibworth Beauchamp,
Leicestershire. LE8 0RX
Tel: 0116 279 2299
Email: books@troubador.co.uk
Web: www.troubador.co.uk/matador
Twitter: @matadorbooks

ISBN 978 1838594 688

British Library Cataloguing in Publication Data.
A catalogue record for this book is available from the British Library.

Printed and bound by CPI Group (UK) Ltd, Croydon, CR0 4YY
Typeset in 11pt Minion Pro by Troubador Publishing Ltd, Leicester, UK

Matador is an imprint of Troubador Publishing Ltd

For my muse

For my captain

For the songs we could have sung

I'll sing them for you

The Prince

This is a story
Of royal regret.
And the tragedy of ambition
That none will forget.

In ancient times, when a young Prince came of age, his parents would often consult with a Sibyl, in the hope of gaining insight into their child's destiny.

Legend had it that these women – living in caves, or forests, or deserts – were able to not only see into the future, but, also, to peer into the very soul of a person too, and advise them on how they might best fulfil their potential.

Now, like all esoteric practices, this coming of age ritual became less common with every passing generation. But, for one particular Queen of the ancient world, the tradition remained absolutely essential.

And so, on the morning of her son's thirteenth birthday, she woke him before the sunrise, telling him to get dressed and prepare himself for a journey into the desert.

It was a trip which the Queen had been planning for years – even from back when the boy's father was still alive.

But, for the young Prince himself, the whole thing was a mystery.

He had no idea where they were going, or why they had to leave in such secrecy.

All he had was his mother's assurances:

"Don't worry. It's a special place we are going."

So, they walked together for five days, in almost complete silence, Deeper and deeper into the barrenness of the desert.

Until, at last, they reached their destination.

*

It was in the lonely heart of the wilderness, where they came to a stop at a strange little campsite.

Here, there was nothing but a circle of stone – a few piles of charred wood – and an old wooden teepee, apparently on the verge of collapse.

But, even so, there was something in the air here – some whisper of evil – which sent a shiver of fear throughout the young Prince's body.

He moved closer to his mother's side, hoping to hold her hand.

But, immediately, she brushed him away again; saying, "Don't be a child."

As a haggard old woman now appeared before them from out of the teepee.

She surveyed the two visitors closely, with glassy eyes and a deep scowl etched on her brow.

Then, without saying a word, the woman beckoned them forward. And, turning on her heels, slowly led them into the shade of her little teepee.

Inside, the space was surprisingly large – with countless dead, or dying, leaves scattered all over the floor.

But, the Sibyl had no possessions. (Not even a chair or a blanket to sit on.)

So, the three of them took their places on the bare desert floor – remaining in silence, until, with another motion of her hands, the Sibyl invited her guests to speak.

The Queen needed no further prompting.

Starting with a ceremonious expression of thanks to the Sibyl for receiving them, she excitedly proceeded into the speech she had been composing for the best part of thirteen years; taking the opportunity to quote from as much ancient literature as she knew, in an attempt to impress the Sibyl with her vast learning.

She spoke at length of the Delphic, Cumean, Erythrean, Persian and Libyan Sibyls of old, and quickly followed this with a detailed account of her own life too, explaining how she had been born into a famous royal dynasty, who had encouraged her to study the ancient mysteries from her earliest childhood.

She then made it on to the main purpose of her journey now; how she was seeking to fulfil the ancient traditions by consulting on her son's destiny.

But, all the while the Queen was speaking, the Sibyl appeared to be paying little attention.

Instead, she had her pale eyes fixed unblinkingly on the young Prince; who sat trembling next to his mother.

Clearly, he was terrified – his eyes constantly darting around from the floor, to the Sibyl, to the floor again.
But the Sibyl's gaze was unrelenting, and remained fixated on the young boy, even long after the Queen had finished her monologue.

"Well…" the Queen said, after a time.
"That is my story, Sibyl.
This is why we have come to you today, for your guidance.
So… what say you?"

Slowly, The Sibyl turned to look again at the Queen.

"I know what it is you seek," she said, flippantly.
"Rest assured – I too am familiar with all the rites you speak of.
And you will know that these are my sisters you speak of.
So… come.

Ask your questions.

The Leaves will bring us answers."

Then, the Sibyl closed her eyes; slowly entering into a trance, as a strange breeze picked up inside the teepee.

For the first time since sitting down, the Queen stole a quick glance towards her frightened son, smiling at him with excited eyes.

"Very well," she said, looking back to the Sibyl.

"Let me first ask you about the boy's talents.
Of course, Sibyl, I am well aware – as all mothers are – that my son here has inherited many gifts from me.
But, though I know him more than perhaps he even knows himself, I also know that the fates will decide his future more than I ever could.
So, I would like to know – which of my son's blessings will have the most significant impact on his life?
What are his greatest talents?
And where will he find most success?"

With each question posed, the mysterious breeze around them became stronger, throwing dead leaves into the air.

Here, again, the young Prince sought refuge next to his mother. And, once again, she pushed him away, with that same admonishment from earlier:

"Stop being a child."

Meanwhile, the Sibyl was stationary, humming some sort of mantra, as a number of the leaves began dancing in the air around her.

It was hard to tell whether she was controlling them or they were controlling her.
But then, in an instant – with her eyes still closed – the Sibyl flung out an arm, plucking a single leaf out of mid-air.

Instantly, the winds ceased.

The Sibyl stopped her humming.
The dancing leaves drifted slowly to the floor.
And the two royals watched as the old woman before them started to run her fingers over the surface of her chosen leaf.

A few moments more and she was ready to reveal its message.

"Yes," the Sibyl said.
"Yes, your son has indeed been born with remarkable blessings.

And which is the most profound?
It seems it is his Sensitivity.
Yes.
Sensitivity and Intelligence.
These are the things which will shape the boy's life.

But, as you know, dear Queen; our greatest strengths may also become greatest weaknesses.
So he must always practise caution too."

The Queen agreed, and thanked the Sibyl for her words.

Of course, she did not really care much for this talk of sensitivity.
But this comment on her son's intelligence seemed a promising one.

So as soon as the Sibyl had discarded the leaf in her hand, the Queen proceeded to her next question.

"Well, then," she said.
"If intelligence is my son's gift, this brings us to my next question.
After all, I would like to ensure that my child does not waste these talents of his.
So, I wonder, in what area will the boy's intelligence find its best use?
You see, before his untimely death, my husband was a renowned leader of men.
Not just at court, but in war too.
The kind of warrior king that even our great Homer would have revered.

But I am wondering, Sibyl.
Will my son follow in his father's footsteps, as is my personal wish?
Will he command our armies?

Will he fight in battles?
Will he be a successful general?"

Once again, the winds started to swell around them, and
the leaves began their little dance.

The Sibyl hummed her mantra; but, this time, the ending
came much faster.
Within moments, the Sibyl caught hold of another of
those leaves.
And as the winds died down, the message came.

"Like his father?
No…
It does not seem so.

This boy is his mother's son.
And, in that,
He will be both greater,
And less great,
Than his father.

Will he fight in wars?
Yes.
Will he face hardships?
Yes, all leaders do.

But, rest assured,
Your son need only to rise on the morning of battle,
And all enemies will fall before him."

The Queen's eyes widened.

Greater than his father!

All enemies falling before him!

"Oh, Sibyl," she exclaimed.
"Please, tell me more.
Does this mean that my son will be a great conqueror?
Will he be a new Achilles, perhaps?
Or an Alexander?

Tell me, please!
Will his name go down in history with those other titans?"

Now, the winds picked up like a tempest, Gaining such force, it seemed the entire teepee would be blown away.

The leaves no longer danced, but violently swirled, like swarms of locusts.
And the two royals ducked for cover, shielding themselves from the attacking leaves; as even the Sibyl in her trance seemed to be struggling to maintain composure.

She threw out a hand – and caught nothing.

She tried again – still nothing.

The storm raged on.
The leaves whirled all around them.

And then, finally…
Striking with both hands this time, the Sibyl found success.

The leaf was examined.
And the message was delivered.

"Eternal fame will surely come.
Both to the *mother*…
And to the son."

Then, in an instant… it was silence.

The winds ceased.
The leaves drifted to the floor once more.

The Sibyl snapped out of her trance.

And, with an exhausted shake of her head, she said:

"No more…
No more.
The leaves have no more answers for you."

*

It took a long time for this period of silence to end for the three of them in the teepee.

The storm had left them all struggling to regain their breath. And the Sibyl in particular looked almost entirely drained of life.

So, they sat there together. Without a word.
Until, eventually, the Sibyl struggled to her feet again and slowly moved to open the entrance flap again.

Clearly her voice had been lost with the winds.
So she returned to making single gestures, indicating to her visitors that it was time for them to leave.

Naturally, the young Prince was the quickest to respond. He leapt to his feet and ran out into the open again, breathing in that evil air of the desert now, as if it were the most fragrant perfume.

And the Queen soon followed behind; so pleased with all the Sibyl had told them that she barely even acknowledged this lack of decorum from her son.

"Forgive him," she said to the Sibyl. "He is just a child!"

But then, just as she was about to step over the threshold, and out into the open, the Sibyl grabbed her by the arm.

In one swift motion, she pulled the Queen close, slipping something into her hand.
And, in a grave whisper, she said:

"For the good of your son, keep this a secret."

*

For the rest of the day, the young Prince would not leave his mother's side. So the Queen tucked the Sibyl's gift into her pocket, and it was not until later that night, when her son had fallen asleep, that she had a chance to properly examine what she had been given.

She knew that it was another one of those curious dead leaves – direct from the Sibyl's floor.
But, was it intended to repeat one of prophecies the Sibyl had already spoken?
Or, would this leaf hold a different message altogether; Perhaps something relating to her own fate?

By the light of the fire, the Queen turned the leaf over and over again in her hands.
But the answers were not forthcoming.

"It must have a message somewhere," she murmured, growing increasingly frustrated.
"Surely the old woman would not just give me a blank leaf…
Would she?"

The Queen continued to strain her eyes.
Feeling just about ready to cast the thing directly into the fire.

And then… suddenly…
She saw it.

A flash of silver. Showing nine words – etched delicately

on the surface of the leaf – which brought a shiver to the Queen's soul.

"Your son is destined to kill a great man."

This was it.
One sentence… nothing more.
This was the last message that the Sibyl was so intent on her seeing.

But with one mystery solved, yet more questions now came.

Your son is destined to kill a great man

Is this a good thing?
Foretelling a victory?

Or is it some kind of warning?

The Queen sat back now, and started to recollect everything else the Sibyl had told her.

"So first…
She tells me that my son will be sensitive and intelligent.
Fine.
Then, she says that he will become a great leader…
Undefeated in battle.
Yes.
And then, that he will win eternal fame.
Fame for himself – and fame for me.

OK.
That is all well enough.

But, if she then tells me that he will kill a great man…

Well, then.
This can only mean one thing!
Whoever this 'great man' is – he must be an enemy.

Yes!

A great king, perhaps. Or an emperor.
That must be it!
Like Aeneas defeating Turnus, my son will conquer another land by killing their great leader.
And, in so doing, he will secure our joint eternal fame, in the founding of a new empire."

Suddenly, the Queen's heart was racing.
These visions were so clear to her now, playing out before her very eyes with such clarity, it was as if the leaf had given her Sibylic powers of her own.

And, in her ecstatic state, she immediately rushed to wake her son.

He needed to hear everything she had now foreseen.

*

From that night on – and for the rest of their long journey

home – the Queen spoke of little else besides these visions of hers.

"It will all be so wonderful," she insisted, as she walked arm in arm with her son, along their past-trodden paths.
"You, my child, will carve our names into the very foundations of history.
You will win the glory of all nations.
A God among men.
And I…
I will be your mother!
The mother of a conqueror!

Ah, if only time were not so slow! These things could come to pass tomorrow.
But, no… patience.
We must have patience.
All things come in their allotted times. And Fate does not make mistakes."

It was as if her whole language had changed, such was her belief that the Sibyl's gift had given her special powers.

Meanwhile, the young Prince just listened in silence, unsure quite what to make of all these new proclamations from his mother.

On one hand they all seemed so farfetched that he struggled to take them seriously.
But, at the same time, he felt an underlying fear in his heart.

Because… what if his mother was right?

In all of his young life so far, the Prince could not remember a single moment when he had dreamt of growing up to be a soldier.
Let alone a conqueror.

The thought of war had always been repulsive to him. After all, his own father had been killed in battle.
Yet, here was his mother, telling him that he was destined for such so-called 'greatness'.

And, as soon as they made it back to their homeland again, the Queen wasted no time for either of them.

She immediately announced the success of their journey to the royal court – and made arrangements to have her son enrolled in the finest military academy.

Perhaps the Prince should have resisted more, defying his mother's wishes or begging to remain at home.

But, no.
There was no possibility of reasoning here.
After all – as the Queen would continually remind him – these were not just her wishes but the wishes of fate.

This was his destiny.

"And no-one can escape their destiny."

*

Thus, the years passed. And the young Prince grew into a young man.

A young soldier.

At eighteen, he fought in his first battle.

At twenty-one, he was a cavalry commander.

At twenty-five, he was a general.

And by twenty-nine, he was the army's supreme commander, leading his men to so many famous victories that his name was now known across the Western world.

In lands previously unheard of, there were statues being carved in the Prince's honour.

And while some claimed that he was Alexander reincarnate…

Others said, "No… he is greater than Alexander."

After all, the Prince had never lost a single battle.

Even when fighting on frontiers where the enemy outnumbered his men by five to one.

He was invincible.

And, as for his mother...

She too had become famous around the world. Though, this was not just for her son's exploits but also for her powers of prophecy.

Time after time, she had predicted her son's victories, leading to her people creating a new title for her of 'the Sibyl Queen'.

And now, after all these years of success, the Prince was marshalling his men on the very outskirts of their empire. On a direct collision course with the other great power of that time.

This was an army originating from the Empire of the rocky north, being led by their own warrior King.

A man who had been the ruler of his own lands for almost forty years; his reputation was arguably even more fearsome than the Prince's. And he too was rumoured to be invincible.

So, throughout the world, there was a sense of anticipation over what would happen when these two titans met.

Most believed that the King of the north would be too powerful for the young Prince.

His lands were too hostile.
His armies too large.

But, none of that mattered for the Sibyl Queen.

From the safety of her palace, she remained adamant that all the odds stacked against her son would only serve to make his victory more spectacular.

"Let them put their entire empire in my child's way," she said to her closest subjects.

"I tell you, he will tear it down single-handed."

And, with such confidence in her son's impending victory, the Queen decided to send him a little gift.

*

It arrived on the eve of battle, as the Prince was dining with his men.

Together they were readying themselves for the coming hardships, eating and drinking like souls who knew that their next meal may well be in hell.

But the Prince himself was sat alone, some way removed from the rest.

Those with keen eyes noted how his complexion seemed darker this night.
More troubled (though, of course, this was understandable, given what the next day had in store for them all).

They hoped that a gift from home might lighten his spirits. Yet, as soon as the messengers presented the little package to their Prince, his face grew darker still. And, within moments, he was seen making a hasty departure from his senior commanders.

"Of course, there is no need for alarm," they assured the men.

"The Prince is tired."

"He has things to prepare."

"He must send thanks for the gift, before the night is over."

These, and a thousand other excuses, were made, so as to ease the hearts of all present that night.

But, in truth, none of the commanders knew where their Prince had gone, nor why he had left in such a hurry, with the whispered words:

"Do not disturb me again this night."

*

Constantly looking over his shoulder, as if there were enemies in every shadow, the Prince rushed back to his private tent.

Safely inside, he knelt down on the floor by his bed.

And, hands shaking, he took out this unwelcome gift again.

It was a box of pure silver, engraved with his family crest of a horse rearing up in battle with a lion.

Inside, he found an auburn leaf – preserved in wax for all these years – with its cursed prophecy now heightened in gold.

"Your son is destined to kill a great man."

Then, attached to the underside of the box was a small piece of parchment, written in his mother's hand.

"Destiny calls, my child. Become all that you were born to be – and make your mother proud."

The Prince read the words – and threw the paper across the floor.

His head dropped into his knees.

*

Morning came. And, in rosy light, the entire camp was now teeming with activity, with last-minute preparations for the battle ahead.

Horses cried. Metal clashed.
Swords were sharpened.
Shields were readied. Orders were announced.
Farewells were exchanged.
Tears were shed in secret.

But, in amongst it all, there was a noticeable unease amongst the men.
Because their leader, the Prince, was still yet to be seen.

"Is he unwell?" they asked each other.
"No. It can't be!"
"Perhaps he is already at the front?"
"Or maybe with the scouts?"
"He seemed fine last night."
"No, he didn't. Something is wrong."
"He has never been this late before."

In the end, two of the Prince's closest generals took it upon themselves to confirm the whereabouts of their beloved leader.

They checked with the scouts – and the night watchmen – and with the messengers.
Then, finally, having checked every corner of the camp, they headed to the Prince's tent, where, moments later, two dreadful cries rang out over the camp.

"Dead!!
Dead!!!
Oh, horror of horrors. *The Prince is dead!*"

Immediately, the camp descended into pandemonium.

This army of disciplined, battle-hardened men now became like a herd of fearful wildebeest, scattering in every direction.

Some broke ranks, proclaiming that Destiny had deserted them, and fled for their lives.

Others simply fell to their knees, beating the earth in agony for their beloved leader.

And still others rushed directly to the Prince's tent, praying that, somehow, it was all just a terrible misunderstanding.

But, no.

The horror was real.

There, in the centre of the royal tent, was their invincible leader.
Hanging by his own rope.

While, on the floor beneath him,
There lay a tiny piece of parchment,
Along with a strange dead leaf.

*

Later that morning, a message of unconditional surrender was dispatched across the battle lines.

The war was over.
The great battle would never be fought.
And, in their grief, the remaining troops began their long march home.

Not as conquerors.

But as coffin bearers.

*

It was many months before they made it back to their homeland.

But bad news flies fast.
And so, when the men did finally enter through their city

gates again, they were met with hordes of mourners, lining the streets all the way to the royal palace.

These poor souls, who had barely believed the rumours until that moment, now watched with teary-eyes, as the Prince's coffin was slowly carried towards his former home.

Here, on the marble steps of the palace.
Under the eyes of the entire kingdom.
The coffin bearers laid their burden down at the feet of their beloved Queen.
As she let out a scream which would forever more echo around her kingdom.

"My child!" she cried.
"Oh, my child.
My… child"

Her eyes lost all life and she fell into the arms of one of the generals.
The same man who had first discovered the Prince on that tragic morning, and had carried his tragic leader on his shoulders ever since.

Like everyone in the kingdom that day, his eyes were flooded with tears.
But still, he held the Queen as tight as he could, and marshalled all the strength he had to offer his hopeless condolences.

"The entire army," he said, "and the entire world – feels your pain, my Queen...

Truly, your son was a great man."

The Rich Man

Truth or lies,
Ignorant or wise,
Rich or poor,
Can we ever be sure?

A Rich Man from a rural community set out on a journey one day in order to track down a wandering Sibyl.

This Sibyl had passed through his hometown very recently – as a stop off on her journey to who knows where. And, though her visit was only short, she had left everyone absolutely amazed by her powers of prophecy.

Everyone… except the Rich Man.

For, you see, he was, by nature, a staunch sceptic. Believing that all so-called Sibyls were nothing but liars and magicians.

And so, in order to prove a point to his loved ones – who all accused him of being too close-minded – he had taken it upon himself now to hunt down this so-called 'Sibyl'.

"She might have fooled all of you," he said, on leaving his family, "but I tell you now, she will not fool me.
I will expose her as a fraud if it is the last thing I do!"

*

So, the Rich Man left his home.
And, fortunately, it was not hard to pick up the Sibyl's trail.

After all, wherever she stopped, her so-called powers attracted attention.
And as the Rich Man journeyed from village to village, it was as if every place had a more fantastical story to tell about the wonders she had performed for them.

Then, finally, he came to a particular town where there were no stories being told.
But, rather, the people were all rushing about in a flurry of excitement.

"She's here!" they cried to one another.
"Have you heard?"
"She's here!"
"Quickly!"
"She's come again!"

And the Rich Man didn't need any psychic powers to sense who they might be talking about.

But, he had to be certain. So, as a group of young men came

hurrying by him, the Rich Man threw out an arm and said,
"Excuse me, gentlemen.
May I just ask… who is here?
Who has come?"

The group were in no mood to stop.
So it was only the youngest of them – an adolescent – who
was kind enough to grant this stranger a few seconds of
his time.

"Why, the Sibyl," he said hurriedly.
"It's the Sibyl who has come again."

Then, off he flew again, desperate to catch up with his
friends.
And, the Rich Man smiled an evil smile.

"Ah. Yes.
I am indeed a better huntsman that I thought."

*

Following the trail of those rushing around him – the
Rich Man made a number of twists and turns through
cobbled streets, before finally emerging into the town's
central piazza, where a large crowd had gathered around a
beautiful young woman.

It was a face he could not forget. The very same he had last
seen in the market place of his own town.

"And how fortunate" he muttered.

I can confront her in view of an audience."

So, he forced his way through to the front of the crowd, and then like a hunter in sight of its prey, he watched as events unfolded before him along exactly the same pattern as they had in his own town.

The Sibyl would point randomly to someone in the crowd, who would proceed to ask her a question (perhaps about a current struggle or a future ambition).

Then, after a few moments of contemplation, the Sibyl would give her response; generally in the form of a riddle or a line of prose, open to multiple interpretations.

The crowd would gasp.

The questioner would give a heartfelt thanks.

And then the whole theatrical process would start all over again.

Only, this time, the Rich Man was determined to make a pantomime of it all.

So, with every question asked, he would mutter to his neighbours:

"There's no good asking her,

She doesn't know!"

And then, every time the Sibyl delivered her answer, he
would heckle her directly, shouting:
"What nonsense!"
"Drivel."
"She's lying."
"Don't believe her."
"She is no more prophet than I am!"

Such interruptions led to a lot of hostility in the crowd
around him.
But, as for the Sibyl herself, she seemed entirely unfazed
by it all.

Of course, she heard every word thrown her way. Yet she
continued to deliver her prophecies as calmly as ever –
without a single glance in the Rich Man's direction.

Then, another question came from the crowd, in which
the enquirer asked whether he and his wife would ever
conceive the child they had been trying to have for so long.

After a moment's meditation, the Sibyl replied:
"Yes.
If you try for a child again this summer, your wife will give
birth by spring."

And, immediately, the Rich Man's voice rang out:
"Oh, come on!
Even I could have told him that!
This is not prophecy.

You are a liar."

And suddenly, the Sibyl turned to face her heckler.
Her eyes ablaze, and a violent scowl coming over her
beautiful face.

"A liar?!" she snapped.
"And who is it making such a strong claim?

I know you, don't I?"

She paused a moment, as if staring deeper into the Rich
Man's soul.

"Yes. Definitely. I know your face.
And I remember your town too.
It was good to me.
Your friends – your family – your neighbours. They were
all good to me.
But you… you still refuse to accept it, don't you?
Even in spite of all that you have seen… all that you have
been told.
Even though all these countless others accept me… still,
you will not."

The Rich Man scoffed.
"I will not accept you, madam, because you are a charlatan.
You claim impossible powers so that these people will
worship you.
But it is all just sleight of hand."

Here, the crowd reared up again. With cries of, "No!", "It's not true!", "Somebody take this man away."

But the Sibyl raised her hands.
"No. Let him stay."

And then looked back to her adversary, shaking her head.

"It is a shame.
Your town – your loved ones – they were all so good to me.
And you… I could help you so much.
I could tell you things… important things.
But you will not believe.
No matter what I say – you will not believe."

"No?" said the Rich Man mockingly.
"All right then. Try me.
You, who are so wise.
Astound me, if you will.
Tell me my fortune – and make me believe."

"Yes!" the crowd exclaimed.
"Show him.
Prove him wrong."

But, strangely, the Sibyl hesitated.

Suddenly, she looked troubled by something.
Her eyes darting back and forth, as if she was trying to recall a misplaced memory.

Whatever thoughts or visions were in her mind at that moment, the crowd could only guess.

But then at last, with a sigh and a pitiful shake of her head, the Sibyl said:

"No.

No – I won't."

Here, the entire crowd seemed to gasp as one.

"You won't?" the Rich Man repeated.

"You mean to say that after all of this – you, great Sibyl, will *not* share your so-called wisdom with me?"

The Sibyl dropped her head, apparently too ashamed to continue looking at the man.

"Come on, now – do not look at the floor," the Rich Man said.

"Look at me.

I am right here.

Look at me – and tell me my fortune."

The Sibyl would not.

"Tell me my fortune!"

Still she remained silent.

"*Tell me my fortune!*"

"*No!*" the Sibyl screamed as tears came streaming out of her darkened eyes.
"No.
I… I can't."

And in that moment, the mood of the entire crowd changed.

All hostility towards the Rich Man and his heckles was replaced by an overriding sense of disbelief.

Could it really be true?
Was the Sibyl really admitting that she could not tell fortunes after all?

The Rich Man grinned his evil grin again, and stepped forward to address the entire crowd now.

"Well, there you have it, good people.
Your great Sibyl.
Unwilling… no, *unable* to tell me my fortune.
And why?
Because she knows that she will fail."

He turned back to the Sibyl.

"You cannot predict the future any more than the rest of us, can you?
It is all a show, isn't it?
Come, now, be honest.
For once in your life."

The Sibyl would not reply.
But no answer is itself an answer.
And the crowd started to grow animated again.

"He was right," they murmured.
"This stranger was right all along."
"She really is a fraud!"
"How dare she come here to trick us all?"

Frustration quickly escalated into anger. And, as the Rich Man happily slipped away, the crowd began throwing stones at the poor woman, who fled for her life.

The Rich Man had never felt more pleased with himself.

*

Following the events in the piazza, the Rich Man headed for a local tavern, where he asked for their most expensive meal and spent the night in their finest room, as celebration for his victory.

Then the following morning, after waking up slowly, he happily headed for the road once more, excited for his return home.

He could picture it now:
Gathering his family and friends all around him, and telling them all about his triumph over the fraudulent Sibyl.

"I will be a hero!" he said to himself.

"The wisest of the wise; to have been immune to her liar's tongue and cheap tricks.

And not only that… but to bring her shame in front of all those people… to transform a hostile crowd into a legion of supporters…

Truly, I'm an alchemist!"

But, while he was immersed in his walking reveries, something happened to this 'alchemist'.

He heard a sound:

The shattering of glass.

And, when he looked down at his feet, he saw that his compass had slipped from his pocket, breaking into a hundred pieces on the floor beneath him.

"Curse it!" the Rich Man cried as he bent down to assess the damage.

"How will I navigate without…

Argh!"

The Rich Man fell back in pain.

He had cut his hand on a shard of the glass – and his heart seemed to shudder, as a tide of blood now started to pulsate out of the wound.

The pain was excruciating, but, even more worryingly, the blood flow would not cease.

And it was all he could do to fashion a bandage out of his

socks, by which time he had lost so much blood that he was feeling lightheaded.

He was forced to lie down.
And, as he rested, he considered turning back around again – to seek medical aid.
But, no. It was too much of a hassle to turn back again.
Besides, the blood was finally starting to congeal now.
And the Rich Man decided it was wiser to just continue along his path for home.

Yes, it would mean walking the rest of his journey by memory.
"But that is no problem," he said to himself.
"I have walked further before without an aid.
And what better guide can I have than the earth and the skies around me?"

Then he let out a little chuckle.

"After all… no other animal in this world requires a compass for navigation, do they?
The birds fly solo.
The fish traverse oceans quite easily.
Why should I be any different?"

So, with his legs still a little unsteady, the Rich Man took up his path again.

And, guided by nothing but the sun over his head, he walked.

*

He walked.
And walked.

And walked.

And, seven days later,
The Rich Man was still lost in the wilderness.

In fact, the landscape around him – down to the last tree
– seemed not to have changed at all,
Meaning that, either he was going around in circles.
Or the wilderness itself had become endless.

Baffled by it all, he stopped again, making camp for the
night in the same spot he had used the previous evening
too.

He dampened some of his hunger with a few bites of his
dwindling supply of stale bread.
And, in that black silence, he found himself gazing
hopelessly up at the heavens above him.

As we know, the Rich Man was not a spiritual man.
In truth, he didn't even know who, or what, he was looking
upwards for.
Yet, in that moment – with all other options expended –
he heard himself praying.

"Can you not send me a sign?
Or a light?
Or something?

Can you not show me which way to go?
Or which star I should be following?
Or, at least, allow me to meet with other travellers, to receive direction?

Please.
Can you not just help me once?"

Suddenly, a sharp noise resounded in the darkness behind him, making the Rich Man jump to his feet.

Was he imagining it?

No… definitely not.

There was… something out there.

Something which sounded very much like…
Footsteps.

"Good heavens!" he exclaimed.
"Is my prayer answered?!

Yes… it is.
I am saved!
Quick. Here.
I am here!

Whoever you are – please help me, I'm lost!"

And, as the pace of those mysterious footsteps quickened, he realised it was not just one person coming to help him. It was a whole group!

The gratitude in the Rich Man's heart was overwhelming.

But, as the figures of five men appeared out of the darkness before him, he realised that this was no answer to his prayers.

These were no friendly travellers coming to his aid.

These men were bandits.
Scouring the wilderness like vultures – and preying on lonely travellers.

Unbeknownst to the Rich Man, these men had been watching him for days.
While he had been walking around in his endless circles.

And, now, they attacked him.
Robbing every last possession he had, down to the very clothes on his back – and then leaving the poor man tied up beside his dying campfire.

"Shall we finish him off?" said one of the bandits.

"No," replied their leader. "Let the wilderness have that pleasure."

*

It was not until the next day, when the heat of the afternoon was at its most intense, that the Rich Man finally regained consciousness again.

He was dehydrated.
Disoriented.
Confused.
Weak.

And the triumph he had won over the Sibyl – just like all the joy with which he had started his journey – now seemed like a lifetime ago.

He had no more desire to brag, or to be praised for his wisdom.
Those dreams had all been spent.

Because here, on the floor of the desert, all he felt was a simple, sorrowful, pining – for the home he would never see again.

He looked up.
And, standing over him, were the ghosts of everyone he had ever loved.
His wife… his parents… his friends.

It was as if they were gazing down on him from a height – or, perhaps, from the edge of his grave.
And yet, they were pleading with him.
"Please. Do not give in.

You are so close.
So very close.

Just one last effort,
And you will be here with us."

And as these words echoed in the air around him, the Rich Man marshalled one last herculean effort.

Suddenly, he started to thrash around on the desert floor, breaking free from the ropes that bound him.

Then, following nothing but sheer gut instinct, he started staggering onwards again.
As the landscape started to change.
And the barren wilderness slowly became grassy fields.
And the endless flat transitioned into rolling hills.

He pressed on, though there was darkness in the corners of his eyes by now.
And, as his stagger slowed to a crawl, the silhouette of familiar rooftops appeared on the horizon ahead of him.

He had made it!

After all this time.
And so much despair.
He was home again.

Home to the people he loved, who would surely nurse him back to health once more.

No, he would never recover the possessions which the bandits had stolen from him.
But surely his strength could return?
Surely his thirst could be quenched?
Surely his life could yet be saved?

These were all the hopes in his heart, as he came to kiss the ground of his beloved town again.

But, alas, something had changed here too.

Was it a tragic accident?
Or an act of violence?
Or a natural disaster?

The Rich Man would never know.

Yet as he fell upon the blood-soaked streets, seeing his former home now reduced to nothing but burning rubble – and corpses on every corner – it was clear that something evil had swept over this place since his departure.

His family were dead.
His dreams, shattered.

And as that dreadful darkness started closing in around him now, the memory of his meeting with the Sibyl came back into his mind again.

That Sibyl, whom he had been so determined to expose as a fraud.

The woman he had hunted, at the expense of his family, his possessions and his life.

Hadn't he asked her to tell him his fortune?

Yes.

That was his demand.

Tell me my fortune.

To which she had replied:
No.
I can't.

And now, as he breathed his last breaths, the Rich Man finally understand why she had responded that way.

She could not tell his fortune.

Because he was to have none.

The Sage

This is the story of Calista.

A young woman, who, for all the world, seemed to have been born into a blessed life.

She was beautiful, intelligent, compassionate, artistic and wealthy beyond measure.

Yet in spite of it all, Calista had lived much of her life so far in a state of deep unhappiness.

Something deep inside of her knew that, no matter how much gold she possessed – or how beautiful she was supposed to be – it was all, essentially, meaningless.

And what she really wished for, more than anything, was the life of a simple renunciate:

To depart from the harshness of the world, and devote the rest of her life to nothing other than studying scripture, and practising meditation.

So, one night, without telling another soul of her plans, she stole away from her beautiful home.

And, all alone, she journeyed to a famous monastery, known to be the residence of a spiritual master.

It was a striking tower of a building, with thick stone walls and long, dark windows.
Standing on this very spot for as long as anyone could remember, it was said to be a place where the spiritual and physical worlds collided – and its current leader, known to outsiders simply as 'The Lady', had a reputation as one of the wisest teachers in the world at that time. (Though she had never been seen in public.)

So, though she was gripped by nerves as she knocked on the building's heavy bronze door, Calista knew that if anywhere could give her the refuge she sought, it was here.

A few seconds later, a young monk of perhaps eighteen or twenty opened up for Calista; smiling at her with such warmth, it was as if they were old friends.

"May I help you?" he said kindly.

And Calista found herself hesitating for a moment.

It was strange.
She had walked so far, with so much time to think about her arrival.
And yet, not once had she considered what to actually say when she met with someone.

So it took a few more awkward moments – and a further prompting of, "Are you OK?" from the young monk – before, at last, Calista stuttered:

"Sorry.
Yes. I'm fine.
I…
I do apologise for arriving at such a strange hour. But…
Would it be possible for me to speak to your principal?

It is quite urgent."

And the young monk graciously stepped aside, saying:

"Ah, of course.
Please, come in.

I will show you the way."

*

The young monk led Calista through candlelit corridors, twisting and turning over polished stone floors.
The building was completely silent. But, it pulsated with a kind of energy, as if the walls were whispering to one another.

A few more turns, and the two of them came to a stop at something of a dead end – where a single door was lying slightly ajar.

Here, the young monk turned to face Calista again, speaking now in a whisper:

"Here we are.
This is Mitera's room.
I'm sure she will be very happy to meet you – so, please, feel free to just go on inside.
There is no need to knock."

Then, he happily set off back the way they came, as Calista was left alone to step nervously into The Lady's room.

It was a modest-sized cell – spartanly furnished, with just a small bed on the right, a wooden table to the left and a red rug in the centre.

But, more than any of that, Calista's eye was immediately drawn to the striking woman sitting cross-legged on the floor.

With her long, flowing grey hair and eyes as radiant as the dawn.

This was The Lady – or 'Mitera' to her students.
And, as she welcomed Calista with a loving grin, once again, Calista felt as if she were being welcomed by family.

It felt as if she had found a home here already.

"Well, good evening." Mitera smiled, as Calista joined her in sitting on the floor.
"Can I get you anything?
Perhaps a cushion to sit on.
Or some water?"

Calista politely shook her head – stuttering:

"No.
That's very kind.
But, no... I'm fine.
Thank you!"

And The Lady clearly sympathised with the poor young girl's nerves.

"Ah, of course you are.
But, please.
There is no need to be nervous, my friend.
Whatever has brought you to us this evening, I am happy you have come.
So, tell me.
How can I help you?"

And, with another of her angelic smiles, Calista felt all her nervousness ease,
As if The Lady's presence alone had the ability to soothe all anxieties.

Thus, she began her story.

Slowly growing in confidence and rediscovering all her usual eloquence.

Starting with her earliest memories of childhood, Calista explained the deep unhappiness she had been living with. This feeling of disconnect; not just from herself, but, also, from everyone and everything around her.

She explained her guilt over having had such a privileged upbringing and how she cursed the very things other people seemed to value most in her; whether that was her beauty, or her wealth, or her place in society.

"It all feels so shallow," Calista said.
"Because what good is beauty, if, in my heart, I feel ugly?
And what good is love, if I do not love myself?
Or fame, if I feel alone?

"What good is wealth,
Or success,
Or any material thing… when none of it brings peace?
And when, all the while, this soul of mine is still in poverty?
It is all just castles in the air.
No good for me at all.

And this is why I have come to you now, my lady.
Though, in truth, I should have come years ago.

I am wondering…

Would you take me a disciple?

Would you let me join your community here – as a renunciate?

And show me how to live a more meaningful life?"

The request seemed to take Mitera by surprise, and she clearly felt unsure how best to respond.

But, before The Lady could say anything, Calista continued:

"Forgive me.

I know this seems rather forward.

But please understand, I have been thinking long and hard over this all for so many years.

And, I swear to you, I am prepared to do whatever is necessary to prove my spiritual sincerity to you.

Just say the words.

I will shave my head.

Or cut my skin.

Or fast until my body breaks.

I will give over all of my possessions to you – down to the last thread of silk, if I have to.

And I promise, I will never have a single regret.

Because, I do not want any 'thing'.

All I want is peace."

Then, Calista fell silent.

She had said everything she could say.

And she watched Mitera's face closely now – knowing that her fate was entirely in The Lady's hands.

On the surface, she did seem impressed by what she had heard. But it was an agonising wait for Calista, until, finally, Mitera said:

"Thank you, my child.
"I admire you for your honesty – and your courage – in sharing so openly.
"And… what can I say?
I am honoured that a person with your sincerity would have such a strong desire to join us here, at this little community.

It is clear you have given this a lot of thought.
And, I have no doubt at all that you could fit in very well…"

Calista's face was lighting up with every word.

Her heart started pounding again, though this time it was not through nerves but sheer elation.

She was just about to say thank you.
But, before she could, The Lady continued,
A strange coldness now creeping into her voice:

"…However, I am afraid that, on reflection, I cannot accept you here.

No… never.

It just will not work."

The words stole all the colour from Calista's face.

"What?
Why?
But you said—"

"No," Mitera cut in sternly.
"This is what I am saying now.
And the decision is final.

I will not take you as a student.
And you cannot join this monastery."

Calista threw herself at the Lady's feet, crying.

"But I'm begging you.
Please.
I will do anything. Anything at all.
Just give me a chance!
Why won't you give me a chance?"

Mitera pushed the young woman back and rang the little
bell which sat at her bedside, repeating again:

"No. It is finished.
It is time for you to leave."

"But I have nowhere else to go!
Please, there must be something—"

"No," Mitera said sternly. "Go home."

And, at that moment, two female monks came into the room, having heard the sound of Mitera's ringing bell.

"Ah. Samsa. Ellie," the Lady said, looking to her two students. "Would you kindly escort this woman outside, please."

The two women replied together: "Yes, Miss."
And forcefully picked Calista up off the floor, dragging her out of the room, back down those candlelit corridors and out into the cold night again.

As helpless as a child, Calista continued to cry.
"Please. I have nowhere else to go."

But her words fell on deaf ears.

She was thrown down on the doorstep. And the two nuns bolted the door behind her.

*

It was a long time before Calista climbed to her feet again. And, when she did, it was a lonely road she now embarked upon, as the sky above her slowly changed from the black of night to the pink slate of morning.

She walked with no purpose, and with no particular direction in mind.

Because all she could do was ask herself, over and over again.

"What just happened?"

What went wrong?

How could she just refuse me like that?

After everything I said…

Everything I shared…

Everything I was prepared to do…

Didn't she say that I was sincere?!

Didn't she say she admired me?

Didn't she say that I would do well in her community?

So how in heaven's name could she then reject me so callously?

How could she just cast me out like that, without a word of explanation?

And not just cast me out, but banish me.

As if my very presence was repulsive to her.

It is not just unfair.

It is heartless."

And, with that, Calista stopped in her tracks.

"Yes. That's exactly what it is!" she said aloud.

"It is cold.

It is cruel.

It is arrogant.

It is heartless.

And if that is the case – then what does it mean?

It means that this 'Mitera' is quite clearly not the sage I thought she was.

She can't be.

Because isn't it true that a real sage is supposed to be a someone of virtue?

Isn't it true that a real sage would never reject someone who came to her so sincerely.
And would never, ever, cast someone out into the night like that?

No.
Real wisdom could never do such a thing.
Real wisdom is compassionate.

And this woman…"

Calista took in a breath, feeling an almost-violent energy now welling up inside of her.

"This woman must be stopped.

People need to know exactly who she is.

In reality, not just in legends.

Yes.

They must be warned.

I will make sure that nobody ever suffers such indignity at her hands again."

*

It was in that moment, with the rising sun, that Calista made a new vow.

She would return to her homeland and draw upon the help of every person she had ever met, in order to spread the word about this horrid monastery and their fraudulent sage.

From political leaders to great orators, dignitaries, teachers, philosophers, and ordinary workers. In no time at all, Calista had marshalled them all to her cause – and, without exception, they all sympathised with what she had been through, agreeing to spread her message to everyone they could.

"Cease all donations to that monastery," they said, "and let the world be aware, The Lady "Mitera", is a fraud."

Yet, even as her message was spreading so forcefully, Calista was not satisfied.

She knew that she needed to do much more than just discourage people from visiting that monastery – and, while sharing her story wherever she could, she realised just how many other people were also experiencing the same struggles with loneliness and a sense of discontent in their own lives.

So, Calista set about trying to help people directly too. First, through staging larger public lectures and, soon enough, in the foundation of her own little spiritual community; built on the grounds of her palatial home.

In a few short years, this expanded into a fully functioning academy – home to the largest library in the world at that time. And, in time, more facilities were built – allowing for them to house and cater for thousands of pilgrims at a time.

But Calista's academy was not just a place for spiritual seekers.

First and foremost, it was a community, where people from all backgrounds were welcomed equally; whether they were homeless in search of shelter, travellers in search of rest or lonely souls in search of friendship.

In time, many more of these academies started springing up too, in lands that Calista had never even heard of before.

And, it was at this point – with her ambitions achieved beyond anything she could ever have imagined – that Calista decided it was time for her to take a little journey again.

*

Everything was exactly as she remembered it from all those years ago.

The towering monastery walls. The dark windows. That doorstep – still stained with her tears.

It was like walking back into her past life.

But, with one change.

Calista was no longer that poor, unhappy, nervous young girl, who had come to this monastery all those years ago in search of peace.

At the door, she was met by a smiling monk – the same young man as before (though he apparently did not recognise Calista).

She asked him if it were possible to meet with The Lady – and, as before, the monk was more than happy to show her the way.

Back through those long, candlelit corridors.

Back to that little room, with the door slightly ajar.

Here, Calista stopped short, struck by the memory of how she had felt last time she had stood on this threshold.

"Am I doing the right thing?" she thought for a moment. "Should I really have come back like this?"

Then, immediately, she told herself.

"Yes.
It must be done."

And, with a deep breath, she stepped into The Lady's cell again, coming face to face with the woman who had haunted her dreams for all these years.

*

Considering how unchanged everything else had been, Calista had half expected to find Mitera still sitting on the floor, in the same spot as she had been last time.

But, to her surprise, she found The Lady propped up in bed.

A grey shell of her former self – the years had clearly not been kind to The Lady.
Her face was gaunt and her hair badly thinned.

Yet, as soon she lay eyes on Calista, the older woman's eyes lit up.
And, in a voice which barely made it across the room, she said:

"Ah – you have returned!
How wonderful."

Calista frowned, as The Lady pointed towards the little wicker chair by her bedside and asked her to take a seat.

"No.
That won't be necessary.
I do not plan to stay here very long."

"Ah, that is a shame." Mitera sighed.
"You know, I do not have many visitors come here these days...
Not like I used to.

But, please. Forgive me.
I am sure you didn't come here to hear about an old woman's loneliness.

So, tell me – what has brought you here again?
To what do I owe this pleasure?"

*

Calista tried to remain composed.
But The Lady's words had riled her.

And scornfully, she replied:

"Pleasure?
No – I can tell you, this is not a visit for pleasure, my lady.
And please, stop with this pathetic act. I know exactly who you are and what you are trying to do.

But the question is, do you know who *I* am?

Well, perhaps I can remind you.

Seven years ago, I sat on this very spot before you.
A mere child.
Scared, insecure – deeply unhappy.

I told you that my life was meaningless.
That I had no place in this world.

I told you that my only desire – my last hope for this life –
was to join this community of yours.
And I asked you.
No, I begged you.
To take me on as your student.

And do you remember what you said?

When I told you that I was willing to move heaven and
earth to join you here.
When I swore I would take on any trial – physical, mental
or spiritual – in order to prove myself.

Do you remember what you said?

You said:
No… Never.
I could never join you here.

And then, you had me tossed out of this place.
As if I were nothing but a filthy rag.

Well, I tell you.

Tonight, I come before you again.

To show you exactly what such a filthy rag is capable of.

You see, I am part of a community of my own now – out there, in the real world.

We work to educate the masses – and we are known the world over; not just as a centre of education, but also of compassion.

Giving homes to the homeless and hope to the hopeless.

We are a sanctuary.

Of a kind which I once, foolishly, hoped to find here.

With you.

But that is beside the point.

I have not created this community in order to compete with the likes of you.

And, whether this set up of yours continues in its strange little way or fades into oblivion… really, I could not care less.

No – I work now entirely for a single purpose.

So that now, when another poor child goes searching for some kind of hope in their life – just as I once did – they will actually find it.

They will never suffer the humiliation, or the heartbreak, that you made me suffer."

And with that, Calista stopped.

She could see that her words had pierced Mitera, who now lay with her eyes closed and a look of anguish over her brow.
And it was at this moment, with all words spoken, that Calista had planned to leave.

She had made her point, and it was clear that her words would echo in this chamber long after she had left.

Yet, for some reason, she felt unable to move.

The weight of all these years had been lifted from her shoulders – but, somehow, it was not enough.

She needed a reaction from The Lady,
Even if that meant hearing her try to justify, cry, lie or argue her innocence.
Surely, she had something more to say?

Slowly, Mitera raised her frail head, and, opening her teary eyes, she looked at Calista with the most profound regret.

"Oh, my child," she said.
"Rest assured, I do indeed remember our last meeting.
In truth, I have thought of little else for these past years.
And I can only express my deepest sympathy
For all the pain it caused you.

But…

If you would like me to apologise, I'm afraid I cannot.

Because you must know.
You were not the only one who had their heart broken that night."

Calista scowled.
"Excuse me?"

"My child." Mitera continued, "The agony that you felt on leaving here…
I also felt, in having to remain.
The loneliness you suffered, I also suffered.
The heartache. The confusion. The tears in the night.
The shattered dreams.
All of it was yours.
And all of it mine.

What – you don't believe me?
You think I would really have wanted to cause you so much agony in rejection?

No.
Nothing could be further from the truth.
Didn't I tell you that you would have fitted in well here?
Didn't I express how honoured I was that you should wish to join us here?
Well, I meant it, my child.
And, believe me, if I could have been selfish in this decision, there would have been no need for any of those silly trials or tribulations you suggested.

In a heartbeat, I would have accepted you.
But…
It wasn't right.

Don't you see?

You were born for so much more than a renunciate's life.
And, clearly, your accomplishments have proven this."

Calista was confused.

"So you are saying that you rejected me, because you knew my future?

Is that what you expect me to believe?"

"Of course not," Mitera replied.
"I never claimed that I could see your future.
But I am saying.
Put yourself in my position.
Suppose a young girl comes to you now.
And she tells you that she wants to escape from life.

Now, you can see that she has beauty, intelligence, grace, compassion… and every single gift needed in order to bring such joy into this world.
But, still, she tells you that she thinks she is worthless.
And that, because of your own example, she wants to throw her life away in favour of a hermit's existence.

In this situation, my child, tell me.
What would you do?

Would you allow the girl to harm herself, and continue with such a delusion at the expense of everything she could be?
Or, would you want her to at least try to use some of what she has been blessed with – even if that means having to, as you say, 'reject' this request she is making of you?"

Calista was torn.

"Well…
No, of course, I wouldn't want her to waste her talents.
But I still would not reject her in such a cruel manner as you did."

"No?" Mitera said. "Then tell me:
What is the best way to reject someone?

Because for me… I think it is impossible in situations like this.
When someone approaches you with their deepest desire… to tell them 'no' is always going to hurt.
No matter if it is said with a kind smile or a cold shake of the head.

And more than that… I'll ask you again:
Suppose I *had* been less firm.

Of course, I could have said something like, 'maybe in the future' or 'not right now'.
But what good would that have done?
I would simply have been leading you on again.
Letting you live under a cloud of uncertainty.

And, year on year, you would have returned here – with yet more suggestions of how you could throw your life away – and doing 'whatever you had to do' in order to achieve my acceptance.
As if my acceptance is something important!

No, I tell you.
A gentle rejection would not have worked.
But I can see what you are thinking.
So let us consider one final option too.

Suppose I had chosen to accept you after all – in the hope that, with time, I would be able to influence you enough to return to your former life.

Would that have been better for either of us?

Or would I have become your puppeteer like this?
Taking away your ability to change your own life – in favour of changing it for you.

No.

That is not the way, my child.

Whether stayed here.
Or returned to the world eventually.
Either way.
Do you think you would have become so independent as now?

Do you think you would still have gone on to accomplish all that you have?

Or was it your agony which has driven you all these years?
That anger, which has been your energy.

Because, to these eyes, my child, I think the answer is clear.
The loss we *both* suffered that night… was very much the world's gain.

And now, you stand before me again.
As radiant and as beautiful as you have always been.
Having used every one of your so-called 'curses' for a greater good.

Your wealth has made others wealthy.
Your wisdom has made others wise.
Your kindness, your compassion – and, yes, even your unhappiness.
All these things have been of benefit to others.

And is this not the ultimate purpose of all our blessings:
To share them?"

Here, Mitera paused, her tears flowing freely now – just as they were from Calista's eyes too.

It was as if The Lady's words had totally disarmed her, and she moved closer to Mitera's bedside, falling down on her knees as The Lady reached out to hold her hand.

"My child," The Lady said, softly.

"Truly, you would have been a wonderful student.

But… please.
Look at what you have become instead.

Not a student.
Not a renunciate.

But a Sage!

The Philosopher King

We hear so often about Sages living far removed from society; heading isolated monasteries or living as wanderers in the desert.

But there is an old story of a certain Sage who, for a time, actually entered political life.

His employer was a young Emperor, who had recently come to power in the ancient south.

Now, in those times – as in these – it was rare for such a powerful man to seek external guidance over how to be a good leader.
And, of course, palace life often comes with far less freedom than monastic life. So, initially, the Sage was very reluctant to take up the Emperor's offer of employment.

But, at the same time, there was something about this young man that seemed unique to the Sage.

He spoke of how his greatest ambition was to become a 'philosopher king'.

And in this, he seemed sincerely willing to do whatever was necessary.

So, after much deliberation, the Sage agreed to help him. At which, the young Emperor exclaimed.

"Ah – you will not regret this!"

And then promised that, if the Sage helped him to achieve his ambitions as a ruler, he would be rewarded with, "So much gold, even Solomon himself would envy you."

Thus, the Sage left his little monastery, took up permanent residence with the Emperor, and began a ten-year working relationship as the Emperor's chief advisor.

*

It would be impossible to relate everything that happened throughout the world over the course of those ten years.

But, as is the case for every generation, these were times of great turbulence and increasing tensions.

There were famines, natural disasters, civil unrest, treatise signed and broken, anxieties, fears… threats of war.

Yet, remarkably, while other empires were being built on blood-stained foundations, the young Emperor of the south forged a different trail for himself.

In every action, he demonstrated the highest virtues. Lifting his entire nation out of their former despair and bringing peace to frontiers which had long been at war.

Of course, no-one knew about his advisor.
The Sage had insisted on remaining in the shadows; only ever meeting with the Emperor in secret.

Yet still, his influence could be seen throughout the empire. Not just in the morality and wisdom of the young Emperor, but also in the way the people increasingly conducted themselves too in following the example of their leader.

As such, in spite of all other events around the world these ten years were a time of great prosperity in the south. And, slowly, the Emperor started being called by a new title, coined by his own people.

'The Philosopher King'.

Thus, on the tenth anniversary of their original agreement, the young Emperor decided it was time to come good on the promise of reward he had made to his advisor all those years ago.

*

It was early in the morning.
And the Emperor met the Sage, as always, in the palace courtyard.

Only, this time, as the Sage approached, he saw his leader standing next to a large wooden trunk.

He gave a quizzical frown and the Emperor laughed.
"Teacher! You didn't think I would forget our anniversary, did you?
You know, it is ten years today since you first entered these palace walls with me.
Doesn't time fly so quickly?
Well, seeing as it is such a momentous occasion – I have something I wanted to discuss with you.
Do you remember that little promise I made to you when we met?"

At this, the Sage glanced again to the box beside the Emperor, his eyes seeming more concerned than excited.

"Yes… I remember," the Sage replied.
"You said something about making me as rich as Solomon.
But, my friend, you must know that I would not hold you to such promises.
You were young. And, in any case, my wealth has come from serving you.
I do not ask for more."

The Emperor shook his head.
"No!
I made a promise, Teacher.
And I intend to keep it."

And here, he lifted the lid of the trunk next to him, revealing the most extraordinary haul of raw diamonds, gold bars, and countless other precious stones, of every colour of the rainbow.

Truly, it was a king's fortune.

"But my only problem," the Emperor continued, "is that this still does not feel enough.
You have served me so well for all these years – and you deserve much more than mere diamonds and gold..."

Once again, the Sage gave an embarrassed shake of his head, insisting that none of this was necessary.

But his modesty fell on deaf ears, as the Emperor drew a small iron key from out of his pocket.

"So, here..." he said with a smile.
"I want you to have this, my teacher.
In fact, look around you.
You see these walls?
Everything here is yours now.
I am dismissing you from my service... and the palace is your own."

The Sage could not have looked more astounded – or more frightened – by what he had just heard.

"Ha! At last, I have made you speechless!" the Emperor laughed.

But come – don't look so unsure.

I will be returning to my ancestral home – which, you know, has been my intention for more than a decade now. And you have more than earnt your place as master of this household here.

Though... I do hope you will allow me to stay with you again here every so often?"

At this, he stepped closer to Sage, who was still too dumbstruck to speak.

And, in embracing his mentor, he said:

"You have helped me so much, teacher. Now, let me help you.

Rest assured, I have arranged everything for your comfort here.

You will be looked after by some of my best men.

And, if it is your desire, perhaps you can re-establish your monastery here.

You could call it a palace ashram... wouldn't that be wonderful?

But whatever you choose please know, there is no pressure... for anything!

If you'd rather just live your days in peace here, that is perfectly fine too.

I want you to have whatever you wish."

"My wish..." the Sage said, in a strangely sorrowful voice. "My friend.

My wish was only ever to help you.

And truly, your kindness is overwhelming.

But I tell you, I have already gained every kind of wealth a man could possibly want in this life.
So, if my time of serving you here is at an end.
Then, really, my only wish would be to just return home again now.

Palace life is not for me – even after ten years.
And, while these diamonds and jewels are so very pretty, I simply wouldn't know what to do with them."

Then, he closed the lid of the wooden trunk and handed the iron key back to the Emperor, who now looked just as dumbstruck as his teacher had been moments ago.

"You… want to go home?" he stuttered.

And the Sage nodded.

"When the work is finished, the workman is no longer needed. And just as no good man would ever accept being under-rewarded for his help… so, no good man should ever accept being over-rewarded either."

Then, with a final embrace, he left the Emperor smiling through his tears.
And would never return to the Palace again.

The Quest for the West

(This excerpt is taken from a traveller's diary, which has been passed down through my family for generations. Apparently the original author's name was Zeno. Although, personally, I am rather sceptical about that.)

You know, I have lived in the East for my entire life so far.

In fact, my whole family are from the East, going back as long as anyone can remember.
And, as far as I've been told, not a single one of them have ever journeyed more than a few miles East of here.

Suffice to say, my forefathers are not a particularly well-travelled bunch.

But, fortunately, I'm not like them.

I always had this adventurous streak, if you know what I mean.
This need to always see what lies 'beyond'.

And so, one day, I gathered my entire family together, and announced that I was leaving home.

Leaving, I said, to go in search of that fabled direction which I had only ever heard about in legend.

West.

Now, of course, this didn't go down too well with my family.

"Don't be so silly," they said.

"There's no such thing as West!"

"And, even if there was… it would be no different there than it is here, in the East."

"Everywhere is just the same as everywhere else."

But, no.

Nothing they had to say could dissuade me from my mission.

My mind was made up.

"And, anyway," I said, "how can you possibly know what else is out there in the world?

With all due respect, you people have lived your whole life in a single direction!"

To this – they had no answer.

So, that very same evening, I set off – all alone – on the most exciting journey I could ever imagine.

A quest for the West!

*

Now, as you can imagine, my path was pretty easy to follow.

I had a little compass in hand, which used to be my grandfather's.
And, with its little dial only able to point East, I figured that as long as I kept travelling in the exact opposite direction to the one it was pointing me in... I would make it to the West in no time.

However, the longer I continued in this rather disconcerting direction, the more frustrating my journey became.

You see, in every village, and every town, and every city I came across, I would talk to everyone I possibly could.
And I would ask them, "Excuse me? Is this the West?"

Of course, the accents we constantly changing.
But, strangely, the replies I received were always the same.

"Oh, no... this isn't the West."
"West is further *that* way, as far as I know."
"Just keep going *that* way."
"We're not the real West."

Honestly, I was baffled by it all.

I had come so far from home already, and was so sure that I was heading in the right sort of direction.

These lands certainly seemed at least a little 'West' from where I had come from.

But you know, I was looking for the real West.

The far West.

And so, I continued onwards.

Coming to yet more villages.

And more towns.

And more cities.

And still, I was meeting the same responses:

"No – you're not there yet."

"There is much more West from here."

"Just keep going *that* way. It's definitely *that* way."

Well…

Evidently, the East was a lot larger than I thought it was!

But, off I went again.

Down another dusty road.

Looking for somewhere which increasingly seemed to be running away from me.

And I tell you, it was like this for years.

I would walk.

Ask questions.

Walk some more.

Catch a couple of hours' rest wherever I could.
And then walk again,
Discovering all kinds of new places along the way.

I saw a lot of beautiful things, too.
And met all kinds of people, whom I might have to talk about more at some point.

But then, after so much time spent in the same frustrating cycle, something even more bizarre happened to me.

I was heading along this one road – as always, carefully watching my compass, to make sure I was going in the right (or, should I say, wrong!) direction.
When, all of a sudden, I looked up.
And found myself looking upon this one little town, which bore a remarkable resemblance to my home.

In fact, it was not just a resemblance.
The place was damn near identical.

And, as I drew nearer and nearer, it became apparent:
This actually *was* my home town.

Now, can you imagine that?

I mean, every single building was entirely familiar.
And almost every face was a friend too. (Though, of course, the passing years had brought with them a few new additions too.)

Then, when I reached my own doorstep, I found my family were all still together – a little older, perhaps, but otherwise pretty much exactly as they had been when I left all those years ago.

Naturally, they were eager to hear how my journey had been.

"Well?!" They said.
"Come on… tell us!"
"What happened?"
"Did you make it to the West?"
"What is it like there?"
"What did they have?"
"What did it look like?"
"Are they very different to us?"

Finally, with a despondent sigh, I replied:
"Well… it pains me to say it.
But…
I'm afraid you were right all along.

There really is no such thing as West.

I mean, I have looked everywhere for it.
Walking for all these years, and asking in every single place I have come to.
But, always, these people just told me to "Keep going *that* way." "West is *that* way."

And in fact . . . you won't believe it.

But even up until only a few days ago – in the very last place I left – they told me that West was "This way."

The next town over.

And yet, having followed their directions exactly, here I am! Back in the East again!"

With that, my family all gasped – and whispered – and, to tell the truth, began to laugh amongst themselves.

"What?"

"Here?"

"They told you that *we* were the West?"

"Ha! How ridiculous!"

"Who are these people?"

"I have never heard anything so absurd in all my life."

"This has always been the East – everyone knows that."

And all I could do was give a resigned nod.

"Yes, I know," I said. "It's all a bit confusing, isn't it?

But... I guess they have just not travelled far enough.

Living their life in the wrong direction.

Or perhaps the East is larger than we think.

Or...

I don't know.

Perhaps this world of ours is just a big old circle, and no-one really knows where they are!

I just don't know.

But, whatever the case may be.
I can tell you this for certain.

I never want to go travelling again!"

Eudemius

Eudemius was the greatest painter of the ancient world. History's first true artist.

Considered divine in his own lifetime, it was said that he had been trained by the Muses themselves. And his paintings were revered the world over; not just by kings and queens, but by everyone who laid eyes upon them.

You see, while other creatives of his generation were scratching marks on cave walls or painting two-dimensional charcoal figures, Eudemius discovered the secrets of colour and three-point perspective – and was a particular master of the human figure; down to the last sinew.

Thus, he was able to paint in a style we would now call 'hyper-realism' more than two thousand years before any other artist achieved the same feat again.

But it was not just his ability as an artist which made Eudemius famous. For he was also known as a man of extraordinary physical beauty too, with his flowing black hair, piercing blue eyes and cheeks as rosy as the dawn.

Everyone who lay eyes on him – whether in real life or in his paintings – fell under his spell.

And yet, for this very reason, people were wary of Eudemius. It could even be said that they feared him, because he was "too beautiful".

And over time, certain rumours started circulating about the poor artist, of how his 'divine' talent was actually better described as *unholy*.

Some claimed that he was a kind of sorcerer, who would imprison you forever in one of his paintings.

Others speculated on his parentage, saying that Eudemius's mother was Hera and his father Hades – hence the artist's unnatural understanding of both heavenly Light and the Shadows of the underworld.

But perhaps the most well-known legend about Eudemius was about what happened when you looked into his eyes.

Because, just as Medusa's gaze could turn a man to stone, so it was said that anyone who looked into Eudemius's eyes for long enough was cursed to fall hopelessly in love with him.

"And it's a love that will drive you insane," they said, "because Eudemius cannot feel normal emotion.

His devotion is only to the gods. He cares nothing for us mortals.

So while you will give up your home, your family, your partners and even your sanity for him… the love will be forever unrequited.

It will be like Tantalus in the underworld.

You will be eternally hungry – and eternally thirsty.

But all food and water will be forever out of your reach.

And how many poor souls have been driven to suicide over such a thing!"

Thus, the people of his home land made sure to stay well clear of Eudemius.

They would gather in their thousands to admire his artwork wherever it was displayed – spending hours together, with eyes transfixed on his masterpiece.

Yet, whenever Eudemius himself was spotted wandering around the marketplace there was panic.

Families would run indoors with their children, terrified to even be in the vicinity of someone so fatally beautiful as this artist.

And, even amongst those who were brave enough to continue with their day, no-one ever dared make eye contact with Eudemius.

So in spite of all his fame, and talent, and divine beauty, Eudemius himself was a tragically lonely soul.

And, what was worse, he could not even understand why the people feared him so much or why no-one would ever make eye contact with him.

Of course, he knew that the people whispered about him. Such is the nature of fame.

But, because no-one ever spoke to him directly, he had no idea what they were saying or what kind of false rumours were circulating about him.

So, poor Eudemius lived his life alone. Isolated in even the largest cities.

And constantly tortured by these same questions:

"What is it?

What is wrong with me?

Why can't these people look at me?

Am I really that hideous?"

Over time, the constant rejection started to take its toll on the artist.

Where he had often worked out in the open air, in the fragile hope that someone might just stop and talk to him one day – slowly, Eudemius became more and more reclusive.

He would only frequent the marketplace three days a week. Then two days a week.

Then once a month.

And, finally, he stopped leaving his home altogether, telling himself:

"It's hopeless.

I cannot go out anymore.

There is something wrong with me.

That much is certain.

Otherwise – why would these people reject me like this?

So – I must find out.

What is it?

Why do they love my work, but not me?

I must find the answer."

It was here that Eudemius started to turn his artist's eyes upon himself. Painting nothing but self-portraits – which, to him, were the only method he had of self analysis, or understanding what exactly could be wrong with him.

He would fill a clay bowl with water; and, for days on end, he would sit staring at his own reflection. Painting every flaw, from every angle… in daylight, moonlight and candlelight… realistically, impressionistically, abstractly, conceptually… inventing styles of painting which, to this day, have never been equalled.

He cut off all his hair, in order to study his skull more clearly.

He starved himself, to better grasp his skeletal structure.

He cut his skin, to analyse the blood in his veins, with its varying shades of red.

And with each painting, he swore all over again that he would not rest, until he had truly seen himself for what he really was.

Yet, still... in spite of all his toil, Eudemius found no answers.

No matter how many angles he tried – or how many masterpieces he completed – the same mysteries remained.

"What is it?

What is wrong with me?

Why am I alone?

What am I missing?"

"What can these other people see, that I can't?

What makes me so repulsive?"

"Why is my art loved, but I am not?"

"What is it?

What is it?

What is it?!!"

In despair, Eudemius lashed out. Throwing his water bowl across the room, and spilling its contents all over the floor.

Then, turning to face the piles of portraits which lay scattered around him, Eudemius violently attacked them too. Disgusted by the very sight of himself.

He had dedicated years to his singular study, portraying himself in a thousand ways: from a beautiful young man to a half-dead skeleton.

And still, it was not enough.

Still, he saw no clearer.

So now, there was nothing else for it.
They must be destroyed.
All of them.

"The wood panels must be shattered.
The linen canvasses must be ripped up.
The pigment must be spoiled.
The brushes must be broken.

Everything must be burnt.
Because what good is art anyway,
When it cannot solve the artist's problem?

What is the use of painting?
Why bother with a thousand pretty pictures,
If not one of them says anything meaningful?

Why offer your art to the world,
When the world does not want you?"

Finally, Eudemius collapsed into a heap on the floor, with the remnants of his former masterpieces now nothing but tatters all around him.

He was breathless.
Holding one last remaining paintbrush in his left hand.
And a knife in his right.

And, in that moment, the thought of one final painting now crept into the artist's shattered mind.

*

It was a cold morning down in the marketplace. And the people, as ever, were mingling here and there.
It had been years since any of them had seen, or heard, of Eudemius. But his name was never far from their lips.
And, as always, rumours were abounding over the reason for his curious absence.
Some said he had gone to work for a famous sultan somewhere in the far east.
While others believed he had gone back to the house of Hades.
But, on that cold morning, all such rumours were to be proven false, when, down by the central fountain, a certain discovery was made.
Or, rather, two discoveries, which would shake the people to their core.

The first was a painting, of a quality which could only have been accomplished by one man.

It was a portrait, of sorts. A silhouette – set in front of a smoke filled, shadowy background, which gave the impression of being either a darkened room, or the interior of a cave.

But, in amongst all this mysterious shade, one element stood out. Two hyper-realistic, piercing-green eyes – which glistened with tears at the very centre of the picture. Truly, it was a window into the abyss.

A disconcerting masterpiece. Both enrapturing and terrifying.

And, in the presence of such genius, the people exclaimed: "It is a Eudemius!

The painting.

It must be by Eudemius!

Yes – look.

There is his signature.

He must have returned from the far east,

Or from Hades.

Has anyone seen him?

I wonder what the figure is looking at!

Look – over there.

What is that?"

No sooner had the question being asked than the rest of the crowd seemed to turn as one.

And, following the line of sight dictated by Eudemius' painting – all attention now came to rest on something else.

A body.
Lying under a marble archway.

His head was shaved.
His skin was like parchment.
And his eyes were empty sockets.
"Who is it?" the people asked, as the bravest among them
moved closer.

In his left hand, the dead man held a paintbrush.
And in his right, he held bloody knife.

And, in that moment, a voice in the crowd cried out:

"It's Eudemius.
Look. The painting…. and the dead man.
Oh, lord… it's Eudemius."

Pitera

In the days when this world was unexplored, there existed a little village in the shadow of the Appalachian mountains.

Comprised mostly of farmers, merchants, artisans and labourers, it was said that this community was originally founded by a great Sage as a place of deep spiritual significance.

But, with the passing of so many generations since then, the present population were rather more secular, content with living simple, unexamined lives.

Thus, the only connection they now had to their past was in folklore.

And the stories of their legendary founder had become nothing but fantasy to most of the villagers.

Pitera was different, though.

For him, these stories were so much more than fiction.

And "the Sage" was a real, historical figure.

Someone the young Pitera hoped to emulate one day.

After all, he and the Sage already had a lot in common.

They were both born into agricultural families and shared an equal love for the natural world.

They were both solitary children, growing up with no real friends.

And, even in appearance, it was said that the Sage was a small, blond-haired boy, with a gap between his front teeth; just like Pitera.

So whenever Pitera's parents told him these stories of the Sage's later life – and all his adventures – the young boy felt as if they were talking about his own future too.

And the adventures he would undertake for himself when he was old enough.

Now, unfortunately, it is not possible for us recount all of the legends about the Sage's life here.

Indeed, it would take many volumes to cover such a life adequately.

But, in short, the general narrative was something like this:

Throughout his childhood, the Sage had constantly insisted to his family that "the mountains were calling him". And so, on his sixteenth birthday, he decided to run away from home, choosing to pursue the life of a hermit somewhere on one of those unexplored peaks.

Here, he spent many years alone; wandering and meditating. Until, eventually, he achieved enlightenment, and decided to return to the world of the living once more, in order to share these deeper realisations.

Initially, he only attracted a few followers. But, slowly, word started to spread. And a whole community started to form around him – with people coming from far and wide to become students of this great teacher.

Now, of course, this had apparently all happened centuries before Pitera was even born.
And, in truth, no-one agreed on exactly what happened next – once the Sage's community had been fully established as its own little village.

Some said that the Sage simply grew old and died peacefully, surrounded by friends and disciples.

Others, in more fantastical versions, suggested that the Sage had actually just returned to the mountains again. And that, to this very day, he was somewhere out there still, watching over them all from afar.

But, whatever the real truth was, for Pitera, the effect was just as profound.
This man was his spirit guide.

So while the rest of his peers slowly moved away from the stories of the Sage – and gave their hearts to other heroes – Pitera remained steadfast in his loyalty to this legendary man.

Continuing to believe that, one day, when he was old enough, he would follow in the Sage's footsteps.

He would leave home pursuing enlightenment out there in the mountains – and, if he was lucky enough, perhaps even becoming the Sage's pupil (if the man did indeed still exist out there somewhere).

However, for now at least, the young boy knew that he had to be patient.

After all, the Sage did not leave his home until he was sixteen years old – and Pitera himself had only just turned fourteen.

So, if he wanted to emulate his hero exactly, he had to wait a little while longer.

"Just two more years," Pitera thought. "Then, my life begins."

*

Well, these two years soon passed.
And as the fateful day approached, Pitera was convinced that his sixteenth birthday would turn him into a man overnight.

He assumed that he would simply wake up that morning physically stronger, mentally sharper and, in every way, more capable of coping with any harshness that the mountains could throw at him.

Yet, when the long-awaited day actually arrived, the reality could not have been more different.

Pitera woke up and felt just the same as he had the day before, as a fifteen-year-old.

His body was still nowhere near developed. (He was considerably smaller, and weaker, than most of his peers – and a long way from reaching the same height as his father.)

And as for his mental development, while the young boy had always been fiercely intelligent, he had to admit that, emotionally, he was still too vulnerable to the harshness of the wild.

Like so many adolescents, he was caught between the desire for independence and the need for his parents' protection.

So, though he still set about packing his bag that morning – by the time afternoon came, Pitera found himself having to face facts.

He was not ready yet.

So, what could be done?

There was no choice but to delay his long-planned departure… if only for another year or two.

It was the hardest decision he had ever made – but, under the circumstance, Pitera knew it was the wisest thing he could do, given the hand fate had dealt to him.

"And if it means that I cannot literally emulate the Sage year for year," he thought.

"Then, at least, I will still be pursuing the same end destination.

Just a few more years, and I know I will be much better prepared for my journey.

And, in fact, to set out when I am a little older may even be to my advantage.

Giving me two years' head start in terms of education or experiences."

Thus, Pitera settled back into his former life.

Still dreaming about the moment of his eventual departure... Just waiting for the right time.

*

A few more years passed, and Pitera turned seventeen.
Then eighteen.
Then nineteen.
Then twenty.

He took up working as a carpenter's apprentice, accepting a role with one of his father's friends.

And, in every way, these four years had transformed him from a boy into a man.

Thinking back on his sixteenth birthday now, Pitera was sure that he had outgrown all of the physical and mental weaknesses which had then stopped him from acting upon his dream.

Yet, for some reason, he still remained at home. Always planning for the day of his departure – but never quite making it there.

Every few months, he would pack a bag – and start actively thinking about following the Sage into the mountains again. But then, each time, a voice inside would tell him: "No… it's not the right time.
There is still too much to take care of."

And he would look again at all the obstacles in his way, to prevent his departure.

First, there was his apprenticeship work, which his father had worked so hard to secure for him.
He had only just made it to halfway through a five-year commitment.
And he could not bear to think how upset his father – or any of his family – would be, if he simply gave it all up in favour of a hermit's life.

At the same time, there was his social life too.
Because, for the first time in his life, Pitera had managed to attract a little friendship group, made up of other young apprentices, just like him.

So, was he really supposed to abandon them all now too, and condemn himself to an even lonelier life than he had

had before?

"No," Pitera said to himself.
"Not yet.
It is just not the right moment.

I can walk my own path any time.
But, just once, I'd like to walk a path with others for a while."

And so, Pitera decided to delay again.
Just for another couple of years.

He would definitely still leave for the mountains 'as soon as he could'.
But, first, he would see out these commitments…
If only for the sake of his father.

He would finish his apprenticeship,
Enjoy a few more years with his friends,
And then, by the time his training was complete,
He would be in a much better position to sit down with everyone and tell them of his next plan.

"That way," he thought, "I will not have to leave home under a cloud.
Rather, I can leave with everyone wishing me luck… which is surely a much better way to go on a quest for enlightenment anyway."

He continued to wait.

Three more years passed, and, by twenty-three, there had been even greater changes in Pitera's life.

His apprenticeship finished, but, almost immediately, he was offered a job working in partnership with a local master, an opportunity which absolutely thrilled Pitera's father, and which Pitera himself felt impossible to turn down.

Then, soon after joining this new workshop, Pitera met Gaia, the only daughter of his new employer.

She sparked a feeling in the young carpenter that he had never known before. And, in no time at all, the two of them married, much to the delight of both families.

From here, they moved into a house just a mile away from Pitera's workshop. And, a year later, were welcoming their first child into the world.
A baby boy, whom they named Ahab – after Pitera's father.

It was now impossible for Pitera to think of anything else besides working and providing for his family.
Not just his wife and son, but also for his ageing parents, who were so very proud of their carpenter son.

The days passed.
The seasons ranged.

The years drifted by, like a mountainous breeze.
And, before he knew it, Pitera found himself at thirty years old.
Living a life which, for all intents and purposes, should have been deeply contented.

Yet still, every so often.
He would catch himself looking over at those mountains again.
And, just like when he was a child, he would still hear them calling to him.
Only, now, their words were scornful.

"You broke your promise," they said.
"You, who were so sure that you wanted to be a Sage.
Didn't you once say that your fate is here, with us?
Didn't you hope for better things?

But, no.
You have chosen somebody else's life."

And they were right.

This was not the life Pitera had wanted.

But, with all these external pressures put upon him,
How could any of it have been different?

*

"Did the Sage ever have to suffer such responsibilities as me?" Pitera lamented, in rare moments of solitude.

"No – his life was so very blessed, wasn't it?

He was able to just up and leave at sixteen – without a care for anyone or anything else.

Whereas, for me…

My life has conspired against me.

"At every juncture, I have been blocked,

Given nothing but complexity after complexity – when all I ever wanted was simplicity!"

And the more he brooded, the more resentful he became.

"My life is a death sentence!

"My home is a prison!

"My family are the chains around my legs!"

And even at work, where his hands were kept so busy, still, Pitera's mind could find no peace.

No matter where he was – he could not escape himself.

And, while working alone in his workshop one stifling afternoon, he suddenly slammed down his tools, and cried out.

"Oh, why did I ever accept that blasted apprenticeship?!!"

"What kind of coward am I, to allow myself to be enslaved like this?

"If I had only left when I was sixteen… then none of this would have happened!
I would have been like the Sage by now.
Or, at least, well on my way to becoming like him.

"Yet, here I am instead.
Wasting away!
Carving my own coffin.
Living everybody else's life – at the expense of my own.

Oh, I could have been…
I would have been…

I *should* have been…"

And, with that, something snapped inside Pitera.

All thoughts of his life, his work, his family and his responsibilities seemed to shatter before his eyes. And a new, half-crazed shadow swept over him.

"*No!!!*" he screamed, slamming his hand onto the table before him.

"No more!
Not another moment of this torture!

I am leaving.

Now."

Then, like a man possessed, he ran out into the open air.

*

The sun was low in the sky as Pitera emerged from his workshop. But he knew that, as long as he did not delay, he would be able to cover at least eight or ten miles before nightfall.

Where he would sleep, what he would eat, or how long it would take him to actually reach the mountains were all questions that did not even enter Pitera's mind in his frenzied state.

All that mattered to him now was to leave.

So off he ran.
Head down.
Heart pounding violently in his throat.

He promised himself that he would not look back.

That his path was set.
And, this time, he could *never* go back.

But, a few miles into his flight, having just made out of the wheat fields which formed the very last borders of his homeland – the carpenter could not resist one final glance of the only land he had ever known.

Hesitantly, he turned again,
And, fighting tears, he looked back at his little village
– seeing it as he had never seen it before, as a lonely
silhouette, on a horizon of amber gold, with little smoke
plumes swirling up into the evening sky.

"My home…" Pitera sighed.
"You have never looked so beautiful."

Then, with a teardrop escaping his eye, he bowed his head.

And, suddenly, he felt a hand grab him by his shoulder.

In terror, Pitera leapt back, instinctively raising his arms,
to protect himself from whatever attacker had ambushed
him.

But, as soon as he laid eyed upon the man who had touched
him, the carpenter stopped short again.

His assailant was just a little old man.
Clearly a tramp or a vagabond, with his ragged clothes and
a face which has seen too many winters.

"Ah, terribly sorry to startle you, my good man," the tramp
said, apologetically.

And Pitera slowly lowered his arms, glaring at the old fool.

"Leave me alone, beggar. I have nothing for you."

"Really?" The tramp smiled.

"Nothing for me, eh?

Well, my friend… rest assured. I am seeking nothing from you!

Only – I'm a little lost out here.

And was wondering if you could spare me a few directions, if you please?

You see, I was under the impression that there is a little village in these parts.

And, if I've heard correctly, the little village is something of a holy place.

Is that right?"

Pitera made no response.

But it seemed not to matter to the beggar, who simply continued cheerfully:

"Well, I must confess, I do not personally believe in such things as holy places.

At least, not in the way they are usually portrayed.

See, I have travelled quite extensively in my years – and, to my mind, all places tend to have a certain amount of holiness to them.

Just like all places have an additional unholiness too – wouldn't you agree?

Ha!

Well, anyway.

Be that as it may.

I have it on good authority that this particular 'holy place' I'm looking for is quite beautiful.

And, they say the people there are renowned for their hospitality.

Which, you will understand, is rather an appealing prospect for an old stranger like myself.

But, you see, this is my problem.

I have been wandering in these parts for many days now... and, for the life of me, I have not been able to locate this little village!

North, east and west, I have found no success.

So I wonder, my young sir, do you happen to know which way I should be going?

Once again, Pitera was wary about responding.

Something about the old tramp seemed a little off. But, at the same time, he didn't like the idea of just leaving the poor man to wander aimlessly out here.

Especially when he was obviously not quite of sound mind.

So, after a few moments' more consideration, Pitera sighed, and said:

"I don't know if it is exactly the holy place you are looking for.

But, if it's a village you are seeking – then, yes, you are in the right area now.

Do you see the smoke over there on the horizon?

If you just continue on this path – due south – you should make it there by nightfall."

At which point, the old man briefly squinted in the direction Pitera was pointing him in.

And then, with a happy laugh, he exclaimed:
"Ah – of course!
Yes, I see it very clearly now.
The smoke.
The horizon.
The south!
It was always the south!!
Ah, thank you, my friend.
You have saved an old man from a lot of unnecessary walking.

But, while we are here…
Would you tell me one more thing?

If the smoke of the south really does lead me to this little village we have been speaking about.
Then, when I am finished with my business there, which direction would I need to follow in order to leave again?
That is to say… which direction would I need to take in order to head from the village into the mountains?"

Pitera frowned – even more convinced now that the old man was insane.

"The mountains are north," he replied.
"Look – they are right there.
Can you not see them?"

The old man turned and let out a hearty laugh again.

"Oh, yes.

Ha!

How silly of me!

Look, there they are.

Right there indeed.

That is good to know.

So, one final check.

The village is this way… in the south.

And the mountains are that way – in the north.

Yes?

Excellent."

Then, for all the world, it looked as if the old man would hurry off again.

But, after only a few paces, he paused once more, and looked back to Pitera.

"Out of curiosity, my friend.

Are you out here looking for some sort of direction too?

I mean, I do not like to pry, of course.

But, seeing as you have helped me find what I am looking for, perhaps I can offer you some help in return?

Or, if you are also heading south, perhaps we can walk together?"

Pitera shook his head.

"No. I know where I'm going, thank you. My direction is north, not south."

The old man looked shocked.

"North?!
Good heavens, you are not heading to the mountains, are you?
At this hour?"

And with that, Pitera became hostile to the old man again.

"That's none of your business."

"No?" said the beggar.
"Well… perhaps not.
Forgive me, my friend.
I mean no offence with my questions.
I am just concerned, that's all.
I mean, the day is already faded.
And I notice that you have no bag on your back, nor supplies in your hand.
So, with the village being as close as you say it is, are you sure that you are following the right path this evening?"

The words seemed innocent enough, but something in the old man's tone struck a nerve with Pitera.

"I know what I'm doing," he replied coldly.
"Now off you go.
That is your route – mine is this way."

And he turned his back on the old man.

Taking up his former path, until he felt the old man grab him from behind again.

"You know, you won't find what you're looking for."

"What?" Pitera snapped.
"And how exactly do you know what I am looking for?"

"Well of course, I do not," the tramp replied.
"But perhaps this is my point.
I don't think you know what you're looking for either."

"Oh, rest assured, I know exactly what I am looking for.
Just leave me alone."

"But is that actually what you want?" the old man pressed.
"You are saying '*leave me alone*', '*leave me alone*'.
But you don't really want to *be* alone.
Do you?"

"Oh, trust me.
I do—"

"I don't believe you," said the old man.
"Your words say one thing. But look… your eyes give you away.
You think this journey of yours is something you must do.
But you don't want to do it, do you?"

Pitera rolled his eyes and turned away again. But, like a flash, the old man grabbed him by the wrist, clinging on tightly.

"Listen!" he hissed. "I am neither aSage nor a Sibyl, but I
see your thoughts. Do you understand?
I know what you are thinking.
You have all of these questions, don't you?
These doubts.
These fears in your heart.
And you believe that the answer to them all lies 'out there'
somewhere.
In the mountains, like some kind of mythological treasure.
But you are wrong."

Pitera scoffed, struggling to escape the old man's iron grip.

"And exactly what would you know about that?"

"What would I know?" the old man cried.
"What sort of a fool are you?!
Look at me.
Just look.
Do you not see?
This is what being alone looks like.
These scars on my cheeks
These creases on my brow
This dirt, this weariness, this pain. . .
This is it.
I am you.
Or, rather, I am what you will become,
If you continue on your way tonight.
What, did you think unhappiness only existed at home, in
that little village of yours?

Did you think that the loneliness and solitude of the mountains would give you peace?

Don't be naïve.

Everything that you find so unbearable in the world of man will be just as unbearable in the world of the mountains.

And whatever excuse you have for not finding peace here, there will be an equal excuse why you can't find peace out there.

Because the war is in you."

Pitera shook his head desperately.

"No...

No, you are wrong!

I know what I am doing.

This is something I have thought about every single day of my life.

My childhood dream. . .

And there are others have walked this path before me—"

"But you are not them!" the beggar cried.

Don't you understand that?

You are you.

And you cannot walk the same path as another.

So... ok. You have been dreaming about this since childhood, have you?

Well, were you so very wise then?

In those days when you could not even tie your own shoes!
Who knows. Perhaps you were.
But tell me.
What has taken you so long then?
You are clearly a long time out of your childhood now, my friend.
So, what has been the delay?
Who did you blame?
Or, rather, who do you still blame?"

"Everything!" Pitera snapped.
"Family . . . friends . . . work . . . life.
Everything has been a barrier for me."

"Nonsense," said the old man.
"There is nothing powerful enough to stand in the way of a man who is truly following his fate.
Not work. Not family. Not friends. Not even all the armies on earth.
Nothing.
He who knows his own mind, acts accordingly – and fate moves out of his way.
But that wasn't the case for you, was it?
These dreams were so nice, I'm sure.
But you always had doubts, didn't you?"

Pitera looked despairingly into the old man's eyes, but couldn't bring himself to respond.

"And you still have doubts, don't you?" the tramp continued, finally releasing Pitera from his grip.

"Otherwise, how could an old man like me have possibly restrained you like this?

Look at the size of me!

Am I really so supernaturally strong as to be able to hold you – a man in the prime of his life – in an inescapable clutch?

Of course not.

This was just another one of your excuses, wasn't it?

Allowing you to say, 'I cannot leave now… the old man is holding my wrist!'"

And he was right.

Pitera realised in that moment that it was never his parents or friends, or wife, or child or career which had blocked his path all these years.

The barrier had been himself.

*

Silence lingered between the two men for a long time, as Pitera's regretful tears fell to the shadowy ground.

The scowl on his face evaporated.

And, like a homesick child, he turned once more, to look at his beloved village again.

"Go home, my friend," the old man said, gently
"Please.
Just go home.

We all have childish dreams.
We all wish for another fate.
But you must stop chasing somebody else's life now.
You know where you belong."

Pitera nodded, feeling as if he could hear the voice of his village now, saying:
"Yes. Come back to us. It's not too late."

He wiped his eyes, and looked back to the old man.

"Who are you?" Pitera asked, as a faint grin now came over the tramp's face again.

"I already told you.
I am who you wanted to become.
The man of the mountains.
The wanderer, without a home.

I am the child who left his home,
And has lived every day since then wondering if he made the right decision.
I am the man who dreams of towns, and people, and work, and family, and friendship, and love – just as you yourself have pined for solitude, and mountains, and caves.
But, my friend, this is the nature of fate.
Every traveller wishes they could walk a different road.

But, in life's great journey, we can only ever follow the path we are given."

Then, shaking Pitera's hand, and touching him affectionately one last time on the shoulder, the old man said:

"So, go on. Get home safely, my friend."

And with that, the old man turned to leave.

But, it was curious.
Because, rather than heading in the direction of the village – where he had previously been heading – now, the old man oriented himself directly towards the mountains, Striding off with the surest of steps.

Piitera called after him.
"Where are you going?
I told you, the village is this way.
You can come back with me."

But the old man would not stop.

Instead, he threw his hand up in a last farewell, and, looking back at Pitera for the last time, he replied:

"My friend.
You are returning to your home.

And I am returning to mine."